MW00898960

Written by Brittney Muller • Illustrated by Megan Jensen

FRY 'EM UP, FRY 'EM UP, Beignet Man!

AMP&RSAND, INC.
Chicago • New Orleans

ISBN 978-099852225-8

Published by
AMPERSAND, INC.
515 Madison Street
New Orleans, Louisiana 70116

719 Clinton Place
River Forest, Illinois 60305

www.ampersandworks.com

Design: David Robson

Printed in U.S.A.

To request a personalized copy or to schedule a book signing/school reading email
brittneymuller1214@gmail.com

Dedication

To my dad, who planted the seed for this adaptation of a classic nursery rhyme,

To my children, who motivated me to write the story,

To my husband, who supported my life-long dream of becoming a published author,

To the friends and family who have offered their love and encouragement,

To my friend, Meg Jensen, for agreeing to illustrate and for so perfectly capturing not only the essence of the story but also the spirit and feeling of our amazing city,

To Jay Roman and the rest of the Café du Monde family for allowing us to feature their New Orleans institution. Your kindness is as bountiful as powdered sugar on an order of beignets.

And to the city that inspired the spirit of the story from the start. There's no place like NOLA!

Hooray! Hooray! It's Saturday! Saturday mornings are my favorite mornings because Saturday mornings are beignet mornings.

When I have been very, very good, mommy takes me to the French Quarter for a breakfast of beignets and chocolate milk. I put on my favorite shrimpin' boots with my favorite alligator pajamas. If it's Mardi Gras time, I wear my favorite catches, too.

Mommy walks with me to the streetcar to catch a breezy ride to our favorite beignet place. On the way, we sing my favorite beignet song.

Fry 'em up, fry 'em up, Beignet Man!
Fry me some beignets as fast as you can!

***Roll 'em up, cut 'em up, fry 'em crispy,
and powder 'em with sugar for mommy and me.***

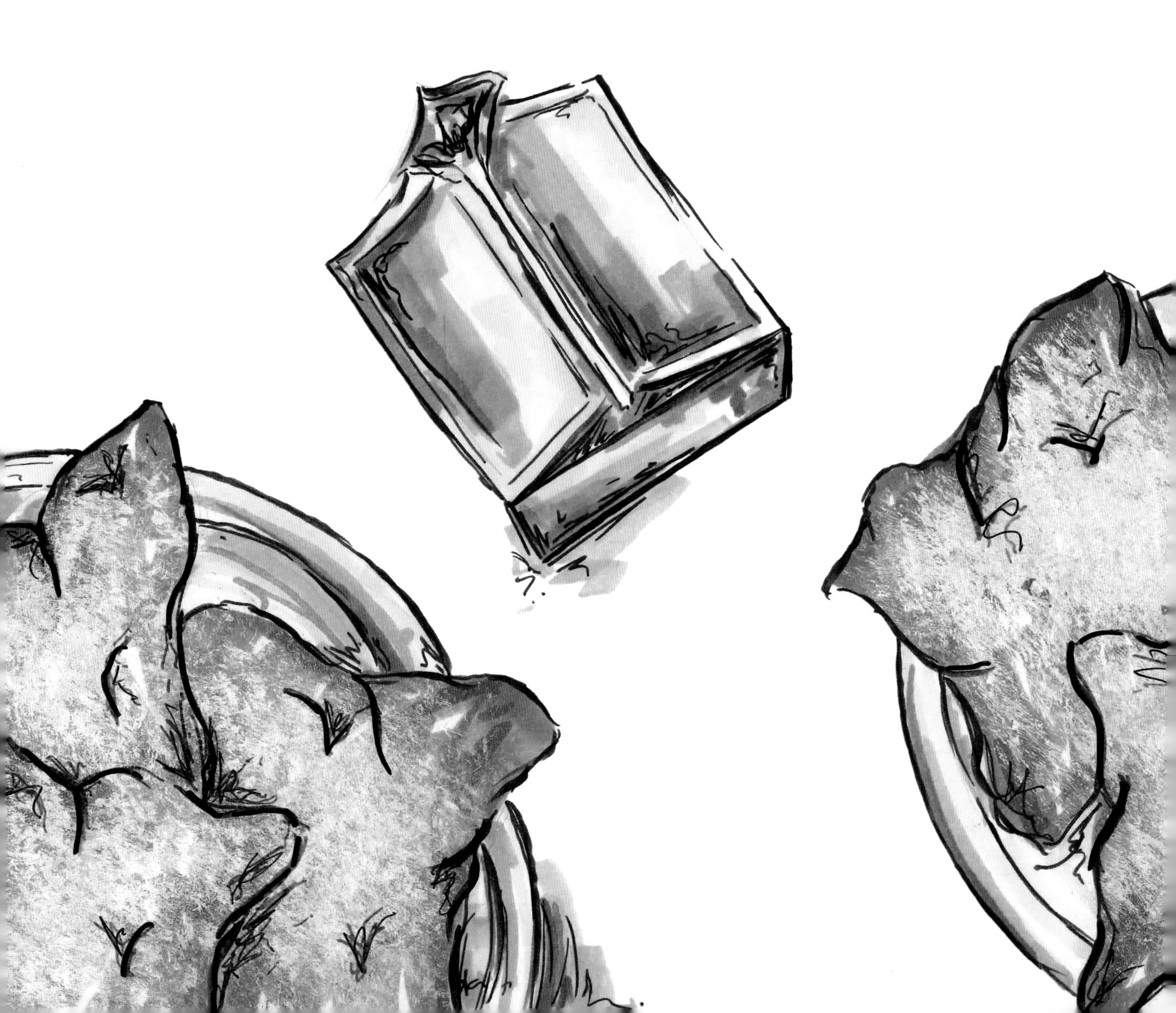

Mine with chocolate milk, hers with au lait
That's the way we eat our beignets!

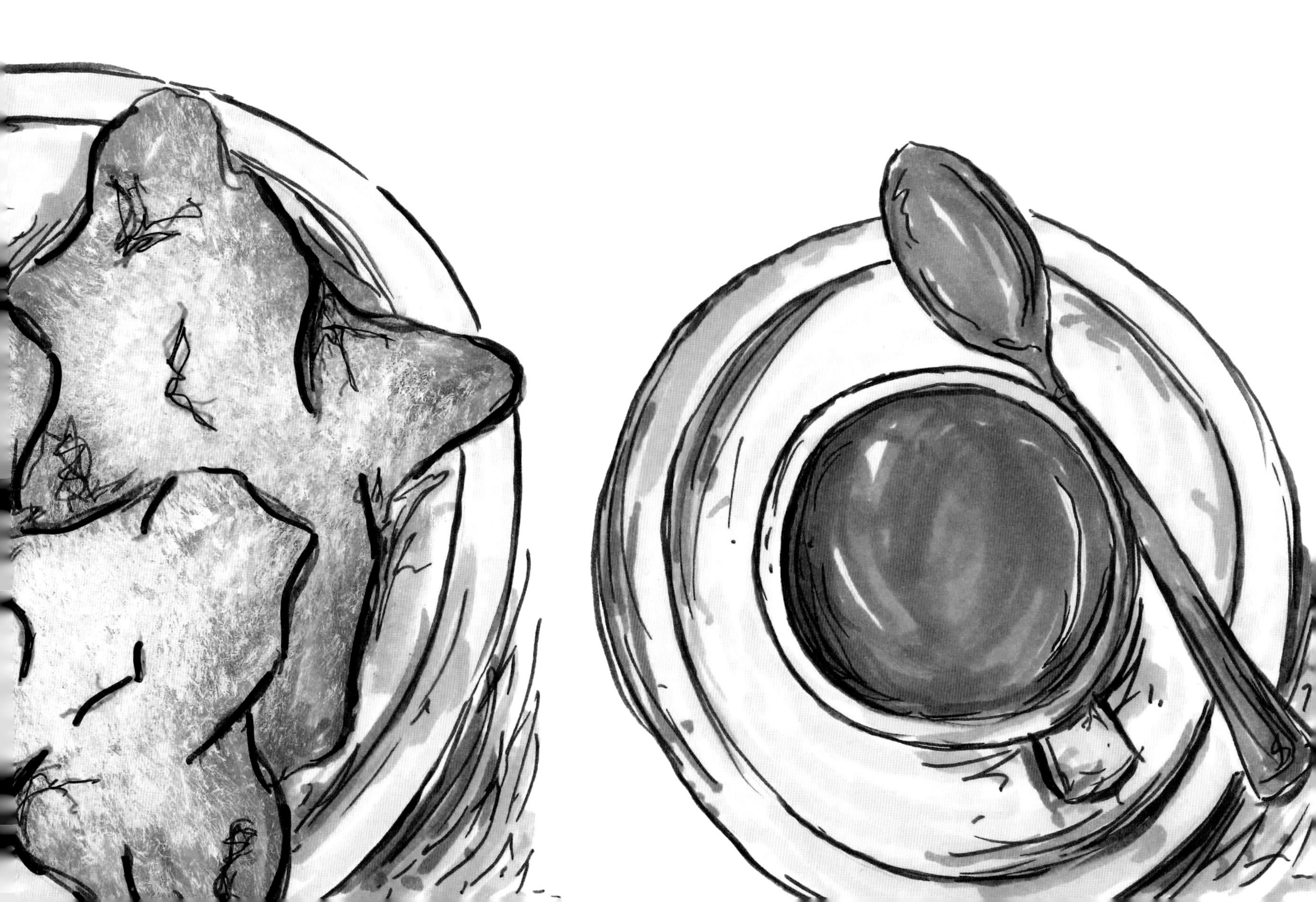

When the streetcar stops, we walk along the River Walk to Café du Monde in the French Market. I watch the big ships on the Mississippi River and wave to the tugboats. When the captains toot their horns back at me it makes me laugh!

I get excited when I see the green and white awning hanging over the sidewalk. We watch the beignet man making a fresh batch of hot beignets. He makes them just like our song says!

CAFE DU MONDE
CAFE

Mommy gets two orders of beignets, chocolate milk for me, and a café au lait for her. We sit at a table near the street and eat our delicious beignets covered with mountains of powdered sugar. Street musicians play jazz just for us!

I clap my hands and sway to the music. Powdered sugar sprinkles all over me, but I don't mind. Sometimes we even have powdered sugar wars.

But mostly we just sit together, listening to the music and watching the people all around us.

CAFE DU MONDE

This is why Saturday mornings are my favorite mornings. Saturday mornings are beignet mornings!

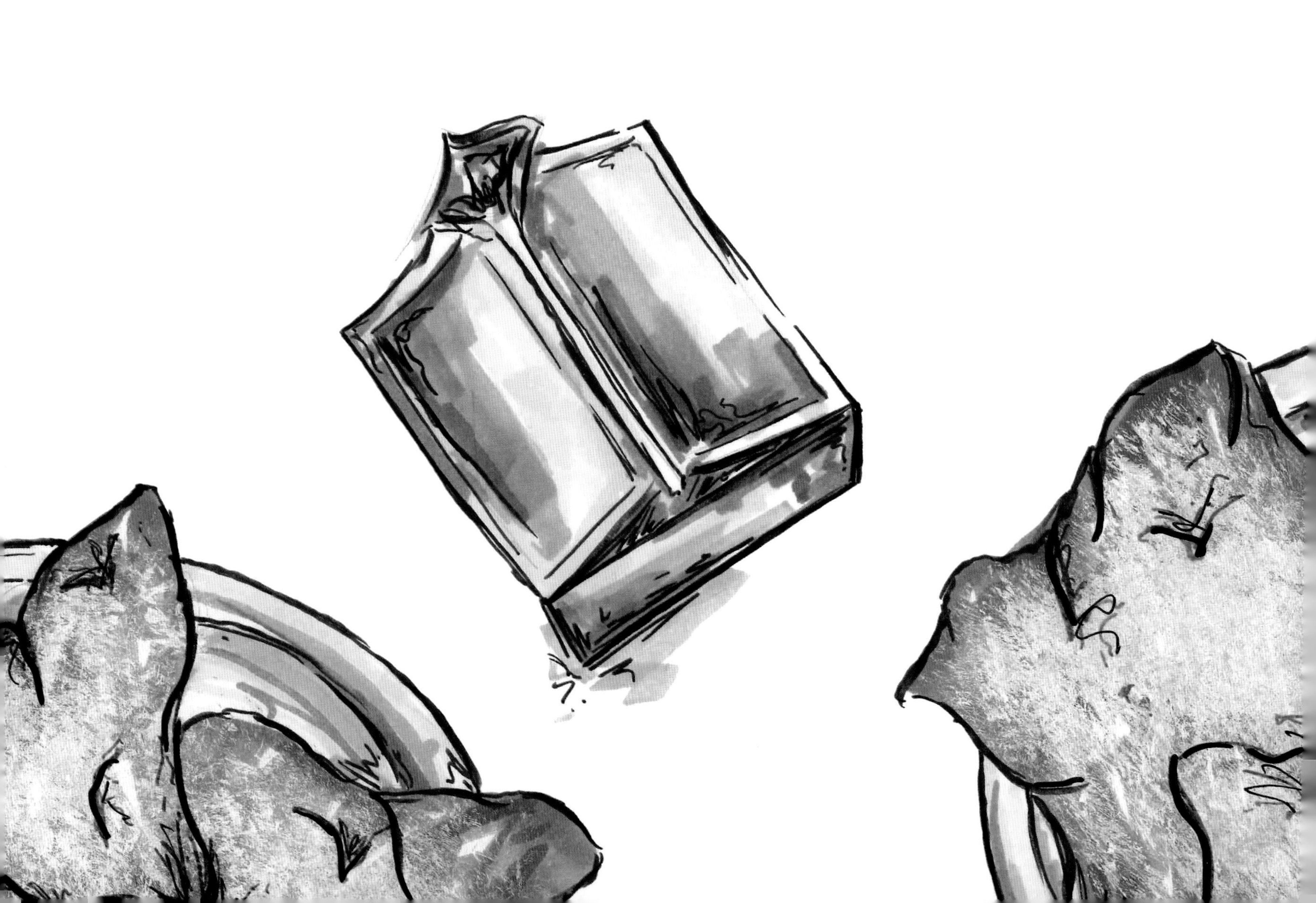

Fry 'em up, fry 'em up, Beignet Man!
Fry me some beignets as fast as you can!
Roll 'em up, cut 'em up, fry 'em crispy,
and powder 'em with sugar for mommy and me.
Mine with chocolate milk, hers with au lait
That's the way we eat our beignets!

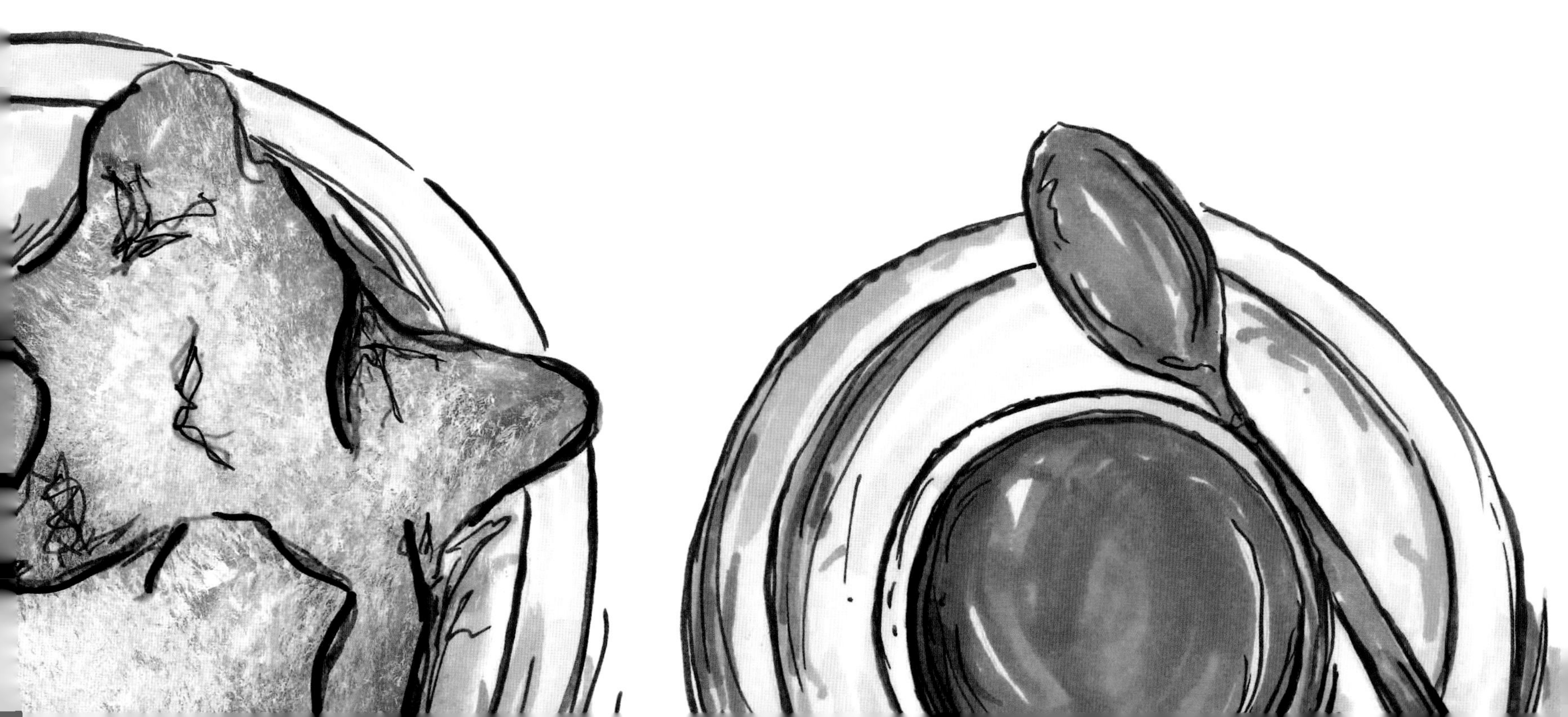

Who was Mother Goose?

Thousands of songs, games, and poems for children have been attributed to a brilliant author known as Mother Goose. Throughout centuries, her works have been passed down from one generation to the next through oral tradition and written word. Such popular nursery rhymes as "Hey, Diddle, Diddle," "Hush Little Baby, Don't Say a Word," "Baa, Baa, Black Sheep," "Ring Around the Rosy," and many more are of Mother Goose origin. She is often credited for inventing the fairy tale genre of literature.

Mother Goose's exact identity is unknown. Some believe that she lived in Boston in the 17th century, but literary historians say this is untrue, largely because Mother Goose can be found in earlier French texts that may date back to as early as the 10th century.

In 1697, Charles Perrault published a collection of rhymes and other folk tales entitled *Tales of My Mother Goose*. It rapidly grew in popularity throughout France. By 1729, Perrault's book had been translated into English by Robert Samber in a volume known as *Histories or Tales of Past Times, Told by Mother Goose*. In 1786, the English translation was brought to the United States where it continued to grow in popularity. Later, John Newbery focused on the nursery rhymes by publishing *Mother Goose's Melody, or, Sonnets for the Cradle*, which helped solidify Mother Goose's association with children's poetry.

Pat-a-Cake

By Mother Goose

Pat-a-cake, pat-a-cake, baker's man,
Bake me a cake, as fast as you can;
Pat it, prick it and mark it with a B,
Put it in the oven for baby and me.

Story History

While playing the traditional Mother Goose rhyme "Pat-a-Cake, Pat-a-Cake, Baker's Man" with my seven month old son, my dad mentioned that he needed a "Beignet Man" instead of a "Baker's Man" because he was a NOLA baby. I thought that sounded like a good idea and came up with my version of the classic rhyme included within this story. When friends started hearing me sing it to Eli, they would ask if I could write it down for them to sing to their children. I thought about what the song meant to me and what I hoped it would reflect for me and Eli someday as he grew, and the story that lies within these pages was created. Through the encouragement of friends and family, I sought a way to share the story with everyone as it tells of an experience to which anyone who has had the pleasure of visiting New Orleans and dining on beignets and coffee in the French Quarter can relate.

Café Du Monde/Beignet History

Café du Monde has been a New Orleans institution since 1862 when it moved into the French Market in the middle of the Civil War, serving patrons and passers-by alike. It quickly became famous for black coffee and café au lait alongside squares of fried dough piled high with powdered sugar. Originally, these golden puffs of goodness were simply called "doughnuts." In 1958 a rebranding campaign gave them the name "beignets" which means "fritter" in French. In 1986 the beignet became the official doughnut of the State of Louisiana.

The coffee served at Café du Monde includes chicory, a roasted endive root which was brought to New Orleans by French settlers in the mid-1800s. Originally chicory was added to stretch short supplies of coffee. To this day the roasted root gives the coffee a uniquely deep, smooth, rich flavor. The classic café au lait is 50% coffee and 50% steamed whole milk, which mellows the flavor of the coffee.

Café du Monde is open 24 hours a day, seven days a week, 364 days a year. Barring a rare hurricane, the restaurant only closes its doors on Christmas Day. The name Café du Monde translates to "coffee of the world," and the institution lives up to that name very well. Since its inception, Café du Monde has been a place where people from every walk of life, culture, and background sit together to enjoy the simple pleasure of a great cup of coffee and chicory with a delicious beignet. A visit to Café du Monde is a rite of passage for tourists and locals alike. It is an experience not soon forgotten and very much worth repeating.

About the Author

Brittney Muller grew up in Madison, Mississippi, but her father's job with the Illinois Central Railroad sent her family on many a trip to the Crescent City. She has always felt that New Orleans is home away from home. She and her Kenner-born husband, Jarrod, met in college and have lived in the greater New Orleans area for the past ten years. They currently have three children—Eli, Penny, a baby on the way, and a fur-baby in a one-eyed Jack Russell Terrier named Desmond. Brittney worked as an educator in St. Charles Parish Public Schools for nine years. Currently she is working from home to spend time with her young, growing family.

About the Illustrator

Megan Jensen was born and raised in the greater New Orleans area and currently lives there with her husband, Andrew, and their two cats, Mu and Little Bit. While earning an Interior Design degree from Louisiana State University she fell in love with hand rendering. This practice gave a more personal and artistic quality to her sketches. Applying this same technique to children's book illustrations results in a loose, playful quality and lively, vibrant expression. Megan has always had a love for New Orleans, and worked to capture the city's art and music with her illustration style.